S.W.I.T.C.H.

SERUM WHICH INSTIGATES TOTAL CELLULAR HIJACK

D0111022

Other books in the S.W.I.T.C.H. series:

S.W.I.T.C.H.

SERUM WHICH INSTIGATES TOTAL CELLULAR HIJACK

Ant Attack

Ali Sparkes

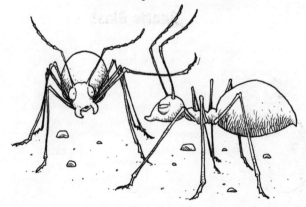

illustrated by
Ross Collins

OXFORD
UNIVERSITY PRESS

OXFORD
UNIVERSITY PRESS

Great Clarendon Street, Oxford OX2 6DP

Oxford University Press is a department of the University of Oxford.
It furthers the University's objective of excellence in research, scholarship,
and education by publishing worldwide in

Oxford   New York

Auckland Cape Town Dar es Salaam Hong Kong Karachi
Kuala Lumpur Madrid Melbourne Mexico City Nairobi
New Delhi Shanghai Taipei Toronto

With offices in

Argentina Austria Brazil Chile Czech Republic France Greece
Guatemala Hungary Italy Japan Poland Portugal Singapore
South Korea Switzerland Thailand Turkey Ukraine Vietnam

Oxford is a registered trade mark of Oxford University Press
in the UK and in certain other countries

Text © Ali Sparkes 2011
Illustrations © Ross Collins
S.W.I.T.C.H. logo designed by Dynamo Ltd

The moral rights of the author have been asserted
Database right Oxford University Press (maker)

First published 2011

British Library Cataloguing in Publication Data
Data available

ISBN: 978-0-19-272935-4
1 3 5 7 9 10 8 6 4 2

Printed in Great Britain

Paper used in the production of this book is a natural,
recyclable product made from wood grown in sustainable forests.
The manufacturing process conforms to the environmental
regulations of the country of origin.

For Katie Ann

Danny and Josh
(and Piddle)

They might be twins but they're NOT the same! Josh loves insects, spiders, beetles and bugs. Danny can't stand them. Anything little with multiple legs freaks him out. So sharing a bedroom with Josh can be ... erm ... interesting. Mind you, they both love putting earwigs in big sister Jenny's pants drawer ...

Danny

- FULL NAME: Danny Phillips
- AGE: 8 years
- HEIGHT: Taller than Josh
- FAVOURITE THING: Skateboarding
- WORST THING: Creepy-crawlies and tidying
- AMBITION: To be a stunt man

Josh

- **FULL NAME:** Josh Phillips
- **AGE:** 8 years
- **HEIGHT:** Taller than Danny
- **FAVOURITE THING:** Collecting insects
- **WORST THING:** Skateboarding
- **AMBITION:** To be an entomologist

Piddle

- **FULL NAME:** Piddle the dog Phillips
- **AGE:** 2 dog years
  (14 in human years)
- **HEIGHT:** Not very
- **FAVOURITE THING:** Chasing sticks
- **WORST THING:** Cats
- **AMBITION:** To bite a squirrel

CONTENTS

Entertaining Tarquin

'Guess what, boys?' Mum peered around the bedroom door with a grin.

Josh and Danny paused in their fight with rolled-up newspaper swords, and smiled innocently at her.

'What?' urged Danny.

The grin got stiffer. 'Tarquin's here to play!' Mum gulped. The looks on her twin sons' faces were so dark, it felt as if Hallowe'en had arrived early.

'*Tarquin*,' said Josh.

'*Here*,' said Danny.

Piddle the dog whined and shot under the bunk bed.

Danny threw down his sword, turned to Josh, opened out his arms and commanded: 'Through the heart. And make it quick.'

'Oh, come on! It'll be *fun*!' said Mum. 'Sshhh! He's coming up the stairs.'

They could clearly hear Tarquin approaching. He appeared to be singing opera.

'But we can't *stand* Tarquin!' hissed Danny, pushing his messy blond hair off his furrowed forehead. 'And you don't even *like* his mum! Remember how snotty she was about you winning the best garden contest?'

Mum sighed and said, in a low voice, 'I've let bygones be bygones! His mum needed help today. She's visiting a sick aunt. We have to look after each other—we're a *community*! Oh—here he is now!'

Tarquin trailed past her into Josh and Danny's room. At seven and a half he was nearly their age but he looked about fifty-five. He was dressed in neatly ironed trousers, a blue shirt, and a proper matching jacket. His hair was severely parted and combed flat to his head. His googly grey eyes narrowed as he examined their room. 'It's rather a mess, isn't it?' he said, in his peculiar high-pitched voice.

'Well, duh!' said Danny. 'It's a boys' room!'

'Yes,' said Tarquin. 'And so is mine. But I still refrain from growing fungus in it.' He eyed a jar of something gooey on the windowsill. The jar had once been filled with tadpoles, which Josh had set free in the garden pond last week. It *had* gone a little furry.

'Have fun, boys,' called Mum, already halfway downstairs.

Tarquin began to wander around, poking at their stuff. He prodded their comics and sniffed.

'*So* childish.'

Danny mouthed '*Childish? Spiderman?*' at Josh and picked up his sword again. Josh frowned at him and shook his head.

'So what do *you* read then, Tarquin?' said Josh, trying hard to sound friendly.

'Oh—*Classical Music Magazine. New Scientist.* You wouldn't know them. I don't suppose you know anything about the arts or science.'

'We know a *lot* about science!' burst out Danny. 'We've had more science in the last six weeks than you've had in your life, you little—'

'Shut up, Danny,' said Josh. He was worried about what his brother might say next. Maybe he would tell Tarquin that he and Josh had been involved with scientific experiments so amazing that every scientist in the world would explode with astonishment if they knew. Maybe he'd boast that they'd been turned into spiders, then flies, and then grasshoppers over this year—after getting tangled up with the brilliant (but quite probably mad) old lady scientist next door.

Petty Potts seemed like a dotty old dear, but

she was in fact a genius. She had created SWITCH spray which could turn any creature into a creepy-crawly. She'd made a drinkable version too, and that was even stronger. What's more, if Josh and Danny managed to help her find the missing parts of her REPTOSWITCH formula, she could change them into alligators or giant pythons! It was a fantastic secret—and Josh was determined that Danny wouldn't blurt it out to Tarquin.

'Oh—don't be offended,' Tarquin was saying now, picking up Josh's magnifying glass from the top of their bookcase and turning it over in one hand. 'My mother says you can't help it that you're not as clever as me. It's not your fault.'

THWACK! Danny brought down his sword, aiming for the back of Tarquin's neatly combed head, but Josh caught it with an upswing of his own sword. '*Stop it!*' he mouthed at Danny as Tarquin put down the magnifying glass and moved on.

'We *do* know quite a lot about science— especially nature,' said Josh. 'We know about creepy-crawlies. Let's take my magnifying glass outside and I'll show you some in the garden if you like.'

Tarquin shuddered. 'Eugh! If you show me a creepy-crawly I'll stamp on it.'

Josh was shocked. He was a great nature lover and had adored all kinds of creepy-crawlies long before he'd ever been one. Even Danny, who wasn't fond of them at all, would never deliberately squash one.

'You can't *tread* on them! That's just stupid!'

'No—sometimes I look at them first,' smirked Tarquin. 'It's quite fun to pull their legs off.'

'It's not fun for *them*!' said Josh, feeling quite hot in the face. He picked up his sword, ready to swing it into Tarquin's head, but this time Danny grabbed it, raised his eyebrows and waggled his finger at his brother.

Tarquin opened the door to their toy cupboard. Then he screamed.

Nasty Little Squirt

Danny and Josh knew to hop quickly out of the way whenever they opened the toy cupboard door, but Tarquin was not trained to handle the danger. The avalanche that engulfed him took him completely by surprise.

He squealed loudly, struggling to sit up in a river of games, books, Lego, Meccano, old soft toys, top trump cards, *Thunderbirds* aircraft, *Thomas the Tank Engine* characters and bits of railway, assorted guns and light sabres, action figures and remote control cars—and quite a few cheesy socks. 'I'LL GET YOU!' warned the talking Action Man.

'Oops! Toy quake!' said Josh, with a delighted smile. The toy cupboard had done exactly what he and Danny had been longing to do. It had smacked Tarquin off his feet and wiped the smug look off his face.

A couple of water pistols bounced out and Danny picked them up. 'Come on,' he said. 'Let's go and play with these outside.' He and Josh ran downstairs without waiting to see if Tarquin was following. They shot through the front door and ran around the side of the house to fill up their water pistols from the outside tap.

'Ah! Josh! Danny!' said a voice above them.

They looked up to see Petty Potts leaning over the low brick wall which separated their two houses, clutching a large net on a pole. 'How are you both since last week's adventure? Any after-effects?' She glanced around shiftily, and then peered closely at them through her dusty spectacles.

'We're fine,' said Josh, putting the stopper into his filled-up water pistol. 'Danny's not rubbing his legs together any more and we've both stopped spitting out brown goo and jumping all over the room when we get nervous.'

'Good, good,' smiled Petty, placing a squirty spray bottle on the wall. 'I was a bit concerned. But you were *splendid* grasshoppers, I have to say! Still on the look-out for the REPTOSWITCH cubes, too, are you? Haven't given up the search, I hope.'

'We're always on the look-out, you know that,' said Josh.

Danny looked warily at the squirty spray bottle. 'What's *that?*' he asked.

'Oh—another SWITCH spray. Very fast acting. Going to try it on some ducks on the pond on the common,' said Petty, airily, tugging at the net. 'I haven't SWITCHed any birds yet. I need a nice strong squirty jet to reach them before they fly off.'

'You should be careful!' warned Josh. 'One day someone's going to catch you doing it!'

'One day, everyone *will* know about my work!' said Petty, puffing her chest out and patting her wavy grey hair. 'I will have a grand exhibition—as soon as it's perfected. After we've found the last three REPTOSWITCH cubes to add to the BUGSWITCH cubes, of course. It'll be much more impressive than you two morphing into grasshoppers. Don't forget you'll be able to try out being an alligator or an anaconda!' She wiggled her eyebrows for effect, like a rather creepy children's entertainer. 'But for now, it has to stay our secret.'

'Joshua! Daniel! Where are you?' came a shrill voice. Uh-oh. Tarquin was in the front garden, looking for them. 'Come *out*, you oafs! If I *have* to join in your stupid game, I want a water pistol too! Get *me* one or I'll tell your mother you're being horrid to me!'

Josh and Danny ran down the side passage and into the back garden, giggling.

Petty Potts stared after them for a moment and then noticed a large pigeon on her driveway. 'Hmmm . . . You might do,' she murmured, edging towards it with her net. Needing both hands free, she left the spray bottle on the wall.

Josh and Danny were ready with the water pistols as Tarquin came trotting out of the side passage into the back garden. As soon as he came into view they let him have both barrels.

'Ooooh! Ooooh! That's not fair!' he whined. Then he ran towards them and squirted them both back.

'Where did you get the water pistol?' spluttered Josh, as he wiped away drips from his face, grinning. He was glad that Tarquin was at least joining in.

'It's not a pistol,' sniffed Tarquin. 'You didn't give me one, did you? But I got you both back anyway! I just used this spray bottle I found on the wall.'

Josh and Danny stared, aghast, at the bottle in Tarquin's hand. Then at each other.

Tarquin, rubbing water out of his eyes, heard Josh wail, 'Oh *no*—not *again*!' But when he opened his eyes, both twins had vanished.

It's a Girl Thing

'Oh great. Just great,' said Josh as he lay on his
back at the bottom of a deep, dark chasm. He did
a quick leg count.

'How many legs this time?' wailed a fearful voice
behind him. 'Please don't say it's eight. Please don't
say it's eight. Please d—'

'Six! It's six!' called back Josh. 'Relax.'

Danny scrambled to his six feet and looked
around the shadowy gorge they had fallen into
when they shrank to creepy-crawly size. Again.
'Where are we?' he whispered and his voice echoed
back quickly off the rocky walls on either side of him.

'And what are we?'

'I reckon we're down in a crack between the
paving slabs,' said Josh. 'So we must be pretty small.'
He turned around to peer at his brother and they

both gave a little shout of shock.

'Eeeuw!'

Each brother was staring at a glossy dark-brown head with small round black eyes and long twitching feelers. Their almost-black bodies were sleek and shiny and made up of three parts—a big oval head with small pincer-like jaws, a little bottle-shaped bit in the middle, from which their six muscular but elegant legs sprouted, and the biggest bit at the back which tapered off into what looked like a sting.

'Wow! We're ants!' breathed Josh. A rich scent wafted around him.

'Could be worse,' gulped Danny. He didn't much like any creepy-crawlies, but definitely coped better with the little six-legged ones.

'This is amazing,' marvelled Josh. 'I mean . . . we're talking—right?'

'Well, obviously,' said Danny, shrugging and turning his feelers up like the palms of his hands.

'But we're not making any noise!'

'Don't be daft! I can hear you,' said Danny.

'No! You only think you can hear me, but I'm actually not talking out loud! Ants can't do that. They talk to each other by making smells and prodding with their feelers!' squeaked Josh, excitedly, prodding Danny with his feelers.

'OK,' said Danny. 'So—I'm not hearing a word you say . . . ? I'm just smelling them.'

'And feeling them!' added Josh with another prod.

'All right,' said Danny, prodding Josh back sharply. 'I get it. But all this sniffy poky chat isn't getting us anywhere. We're tiny insects—again! And you know that every time we turn into tiny insects, something tries to eat us.' He looked fearfully up and down the narrow dark gorge, but it seemed to be deserted.

'I'll tell you what else is weird!' said Josh, suddenly turning around in a circle, looking back down his new body.

'What?' said Danny. 'What could possibly be more weird than turning into an ant?'

'Well . . . um . . . ' Josh stared at Danny and his feelers shuddered. 'We're not just ants. We've changed a little bit more than that.'

'What are you on about?' Danny poked Josh between the eyes with one feeler. 'Get to the point before something decides we're its mid-morning snack!'

'We're girls.'

Danny staggered backwards. 'You what?'

'You heard me. We're not boys now. We're girls. Check it out!' He pointed over his shoulder with his front right leg. 'No wings!'

'But we're ants! Not flies.'

'Ah—but if we were boy ants we'd have wings. All the other ants are girls. Even soldier ants are girls.'

'Oh great,' muttered Danny, peering back over his own shoulder now. 'Are you sure? I mean, couldn't there be wings tucked inside somewhere?'

'Nah—that's beetles. Face it, Dan, we're ants and we're girl ants.'

'I'm never going to forgive Petty Potts for this!' Danny spat. 'And if you ever tell anyone . . .'

He stopped dead, suddenly picking up a vibrating sensation. Josh was looking scared. 'What's that?' he whispered.

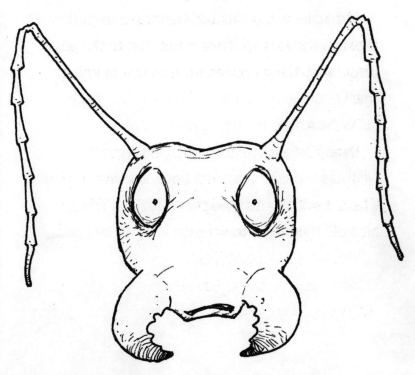

He and Danny peered along the narrow chasm. They could feel warm air blowing against their feelers and there was a strong smell. To Danny, it was a bit like the time when they'd gone on the London Underground. While waiting in the station, they'd noticed the weird warm wind coming out of the tunnel just before the tube train hurtled through.

'Something's coming!' squeaked Josh. 'Something fast and big!'

The vibrations seemed deafening—even if they couldn't actually hear them—and the smell was very strong. Danny scrambled up the wall into a small alcove and then reached down and grabbed Josh's head with his strong jaws.

'WHOO-AAH!' shrieked Josh, his legs flapping wildly as something hurtled along towards him like a runaway train. 'It's going to hit me! It's going to hit me!' Then his screams were abruptly stopped.

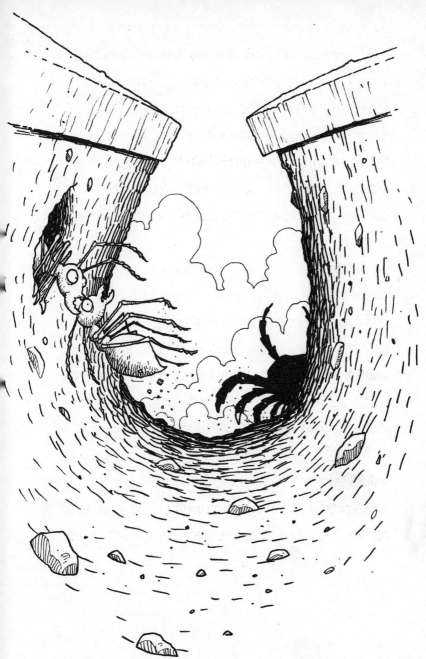

Fast Train to Munchville

Josh's breath was bashed out of him as he flipped up and over. Below him the thundering got even more intense and there was a blur of red. He found himself suddenly upside-down next to Danny, who was still biting his brother's head, scared to let go as the air around them rushed along and tried to suck them out of their alcove.

'It's a train! A tube train!' squawked Josh, even though he knew it couldn't be.

'No—it's something worse,' said Danny. 'Tube trains don't ever try to eat you. But I bet that would!'

'Danny! O-ow! Do you mind?' said Josh and Danny at last un-bit him. Josh looked down to see the blur of red slowing down and now he could make out legs. Lots of legs, on either side of a long, glistening segmented body. 'It's a centipede!' he whispered.

'Looks like a millipede to me!' replied Danny. 'All those legs!'

'I wish it was,' groaned Josh. 'Millipedes are vegetarians. But that's a centipede all right. You can tell by the way its legs are quite long and its body is in segments. And the long leggy things at the back.' As he said this, the long leggy things swept past below them and Josh heaved a sigh of relief.

Then he sucked it all back in again as the centipede slowed to a halt, its long back legs twitching, and then, slowly, began to creep backwards.

'Oh no,' groaned Danny. 'This is not good. This is so not good! Do they—do they eat ants?'

'Yep,' gulped Josh. 'They're the most incredible hunters. They've got poison fangs and they go for anything that moves—even each other.'

The red train below them was still backing up. Leg after leg rippled backwards and then a reddish brown face suddenly lurched up at them, its fangs quivering. Danny and Josh didn't wait to say hello.

Instinctively they swung around and shot
something out of their abdomens into the
centipede's face. The creature flinched backwards
with an angry grunt, and then they took off along
the wall as fast at their six legs would carry them.

'GO! GO! GO! GO!' squeaked Danny as Josh's
berry-shaped backside scooted along in front of
him. It took him several seconds to realize that
he and Josh were both running sideways, along
the wall.

He also realized that the centipede wasn't
chasing them. 'Hey! Hey, Josh!' he shouted—

37

although he knew it wasn't really a shout at all, just a waft of some kind of whiffy chemical. 'We've got away! We did it!'

Josh turned round on the wall and stared back along the gorge. It was true. The centipede was gone. 'Ha!' said Josh. 'He didn't much like a bit of acid in the face!'

'What—you mean we just kind of weed acid?' Danny waggled his feelers excitedly as they reached a corner where some sunlight shafted in and a clump of large furry green leaves with some heavy bell-shaped purple flowers grew. 'How cool is that? Killer wee!'

'Formic acid,' said Josh. 'Look—see what happens when I do this.' He aimed his backside at one of the flowers and squirted out some more. The petals shook as the jet of liquid hit them, and then they began to change colour—from purple to pink, to a paler pink. 'See,' said Josh. 'It makes them change colour. Acid. Ant defence!'

Danny clapped his feelers together. 'Ants are brilliant!' he giggled. Then he remembered he was a girl. He stopped giggling.

'This is serious, though,' said Josh. 'Of all the things we've been so far, this is the tiniest. We're going to get eaten or squashed at any moment. We have to get back to being human again.'

'Well,' said Danny. 'We know SWITCH spray is temporary. We just need a safe place to hide until we change back again. Or should we try to get to Petty?'

'She'll never see us!' said Josh. 'She could hardly see us when we were grasshoppers.' He looked around. 'I think we're down between the paving slabs by the greenhouse. There's loads of ants around there—always building those little crumbly nests.'

'We should find them!' said Danny. 'There's safety in numbers!' He ran up the wall and straight over the top. Josh raced after him. He wondered how long they'd take to find a real, proper ant!

As he popped his head up over the crumbly grey edge of the paving slab he stopped wondering. It was like stepping on to the motorway at rush hour. There, in a huge, endless, non-stop queue, rushing across the slab, were hundreds of ants.

And he had no idea which one was Danny.

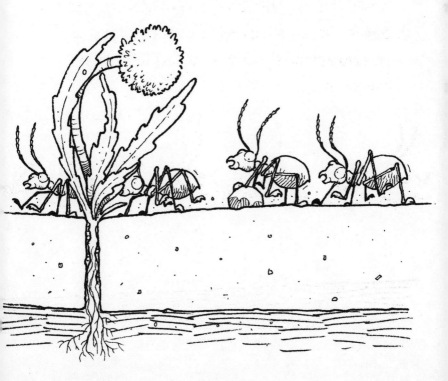

Pop

'DANNY! DANNY!' bawled Josh, his feelers and
his scent squirting gear going like the clappers.
'WHERE ARE YOU?'

A dark brown head turned to look at him, its
feelers waving with interest. And then another one.
And another one. At least forty ants in the long
line were now peering back at him. 'On,' said the
nearest one.

'You what?' said Josh.

'On,' the ant repeated, rather impatiently waving
her feelers back in the direction that the ant queue
was travelling. 'Must feed young.'

'Look—yes—of course,' said Josh scuttling up
next to the ant. 'But I'm trying to find my brother!'

The ant gave him a blank look. 'I mean—sister,'
gulped Josh. The ant ignored him and just walked on.

'Another ant—like me,' said Josh, desperately, walking alongside her. 'We're not from here . . .'

The ant turned to stare at him. 'Not from us?' she said. 'Not?'

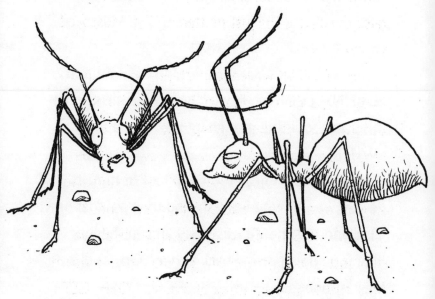

Josh suddenly remembered something from one of his insect books. Something important. Ants did not like ants from different colonies. Not at all. It was murder if someone came to visit. Really. Murder. If this colony found out that he and Danny were strangers, they'd pull them to pieces.

'Yes—yes—of course, from us!' Josh gabbled. 'We're all family here!' He heard himself give a nervous titter. He was quite certain that no normal ant ever tittered. He must get a grip. He stepped away and let the suspicious ant walk on. Fortunately he must smell OK, because she didn't raise the alarm. She just muttered: 'On. Must feed young.'

'DANNEEEE!' wailed Josh, staring around him at the huge alien world their back garden had become, with its rockery now looming up like Mount Everest, small shrubs now towering over him like giant redwood trees, and the paving slab as wide as a football pitch. 'Where are you?'

'JOSH! JOSH!' hissed an excited voice above him. Josh stared up and saw Danny hanging down from the thick green trunk of a bush. 'JOSH, GET UP HERE! IT'S BRILLIANT!'

'What is?' spluttered Josh, but Danny just hung down on his back four legs and grabbed Josh with his jaws and forelegs and swung him up onto the slanting green stalk alongside him. 'Will you stop that?' complained Josh. 'I'm not a football!'

'No, but you're ever so easy to carry!' said Danny. 'I'm super strong, I am!'

'Yep,' said Josh. 'Ants are. They can carry up to fifty times their own weight.' He grabbed hold of Danny now, with his own jaws and forelegs, and waved his brother easily up in the air to make his point. Two or three other ants travelled past them along the green stalk, but none of them paid any attention to Josh and Danny's circus act.

'All right, all right!' muttered Danny. 'Put me down. And now come and see this!' He jumped

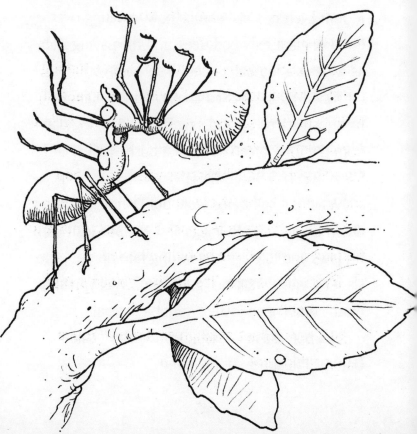

back onto the green stalk, which was spongy and slightly sticky under their feet, and ran up it.

Josh could smell something wonderful. It reminded him of the smell at a fair—candy floss! Hot, sweet, candy floss. He hurried after Danny.

Danny had slowed down and seemed to be cuddling something small, green and slightly see through. 'It's so sweet!' crooned Danny, just like a girl with a kitten.

Josh sighed. They *were* girls, he kept remembering.

'Looook! So sweeeet!' went on Danny, turning the little green creature so it could look up at Josh with its round black eyes. It waved its small feelers in a friendly way as Danny stroked its back with his own antennae. Then there was a small pop and a shiny blob of sticky stuff suddenly oozed out of the little creature's back end. Danny made a slurping noise and the blob disappeared.

'Try it!' he gurgled. 'It's just like golden syrup! Really sweet!'

Josh gave a hoot of laughter. 'Danny! You're eating aphid poo!'

'I know! I know!' gasped Danny. 'How disgusting is that? But they were all at it.' He nodded to the other ants around them, also stroking and cuddling the little green aphids and eating the substance that squished out of them.

'And it smelt so good, I just had to try it. And you know, they are cute!' His little aphid gazed up at him and made a gentle burbling noise.

'I think they call it honeydew,' said Josh, picking up an aphid of his own now. This one also burbled gently and gazed up at him. 'They drink the sugary stuff out of the plant and poo it out again—and it's just like a big drop of treacle. Ants love it.'

He gave the aphid a friendly pat and a rub and—pop—out came a shiny ball of syrupy goo. It did smell fantastic. Josh slurped it up and

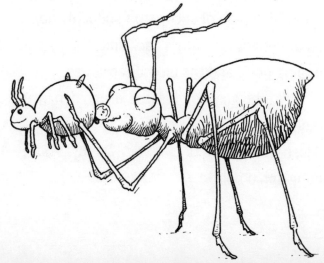

put the aphid down again. He felt sugar energy rush through him. 'Look, this is all very nice,' he said, with a hiccup, 'but we've still got to find somewhere safe to hide until the SWITCH spray wears off. Come on—let's get into the sandpit, and hide there. There won't be many bugs in it because Mum changed the sand just this morning. It should be quite safe. We can hide under a few chunks of sand, out of view of predators, until we go back to being human.'

'OK, I've had enough aphid poo now, anyway. Bye-bye, Alfie!' Danny put the little green creature back onto the stalk. They scrambled back down, passing several other ants climbing up. 'They don't say much do they?' said Danny.

'No. Not big talkers,' said Josh. 'Some experts say they're just like one big living thing with millions of parts, working together. So they all think and say the same thing.'

'What—like that?' asked Danny, as they rejoined the long ant motorway and heard the endless chant: 'On. Must feed young. On. Must feed young. On . . . '

'Yeah,' said Josh. 'Like that. It's like they've got no will of their own.' He found himself falling into step with the long queue of marching insects and Danny stepped in behind him.

'On. Must feed young,' said Danny, in the same robotic sort of voice as the others.

'We'll travel with them for a while,' said Josh. 'It's safer—but we can go off when we get to the end of the paving slabs and head for the sandpit.'

'On,' said Danny.

'All right?' said Josh.

'Must feed young,' said Danny.

'OK, very funny!' Josh glanced over his shiny shoulder and saw that Danny was marching exactly in time with the ants around him. 'Over to the sandpit as soon as we can, right?'

'Must feed young,' said Danny.

'Stop messing around! This is serious!' squawked Josh.

'On,' said Danny.

Josh wanted to give his brother a telling off. But the words didn't come out right. 'On,' he said, turning his head back towards the front and marching in step with all the others. 'Must feed young.'

'Must feed young,' agreed Danny.

'Must feed young,' said the other 1,124 ants sharing their journey.

Happy Ant Day

'YOU'RE JUST ROTTERS! THE PAIR OF YOU!' shouted Tarquin, shaking the squirty spray bottle and stamping his foot. 'COME OUT OF HIDING— OR I'LL TELL YOUR MUM! I WILL.'

Still there was no movement or sound around the garden. Tarquin had already looked behind or under everything he could see, and there was no sign of Josh or Danny. He knew they were playing a trick on him. Maybe they'd gone next door into that old lady's garden. They'd dropped their water pistols on the ground, so at least they weren't planning another ambush, but maybe they'd got something else to throw or squirt at him and were just waiting for him to climb up and put his head over the wooden fence.

'WELL, I'M NOT PLAYING, ANY MORE!'

stropped Tarquin. He turned and stomped back along the side passage, just as the old lady from next door was walking back down it on her side of the wall. As she passed him she gave a shout, reached over the wall and scooped the squirty spray bottle out of his hand.

'What are you doing with my bottle?' she demanded.

'Nothing!' snapped Tarquin. 'Not any more! I only got the chance to give them both one squirt before they ran away and hid.'

Petty Potts grabbed him by the ear. 'You did what?'

'Owww! I told you! I just squirted at them once. What's the fuss? It was only a bit of water.'

Petty glared at him angrily and said, 'It was *my* bit of water, and you had no business stealing it!'

'Well, how was I to know?' whined Tarquin and she let him go, looking very worried.

'They disappeared, you say?'

'Yes, they must have run off and hid while I was wiping water out of my eyes.'

'Oh dear. Oh dear, oh dear, oh dear,' said Petty. She bit her lip.

'Batty old trout,' muttered Tarquin as he made his escape down the passage and ran back round through the front door.

Inside the house, Piddle the dog heard him coming and scrabbled into the front room and behind the sofa with another whine. Tarquin stamped up the stairs and went to find something to play with in Josh and Danny's room. There wasn't much he liked—he wasn't into all that stupid Lego or those silly battling card games. But he picked up the magnifying glass and decided to take it into the garden. The sun was shining and he was in the mood for a particularly nasty game.

It was warm in the ants' nest and filled with 'home' and 'family' smells. These smells instructed the family to do all kinds of things—feed the young, mend broken walls, look after the queen, go out and forage for food and so on. Once they were in the nest Danny and Josh got a bit confused. The ants weren't all chanting the same thing any more—there were loads of different chants and instructions going on.

Josh turned round and stared at Danny. After just standing there, waggling his feelers for a few seconds, while ants streamed past him in all directions, he finally said, 'Danny! What are we doing here? Why did we follow the others in?'

'I don't know,' said Danny with a shrug, staring around at the complicated brown-walled tunnels which led off at every angle. Knotty roots dangled here and there and seemed to hold all the chunks of soil and grit together. 'It seemed like a good idea at the time.'

'Well, it's not a good idea now!' said Josh, looking around at the endless traffic of super-busy ants. Even though there were huge numbers of them, they never seemed to bump into each other, not even the ones walking upside down on the ceiling. 'We've got to get out of here and get to the sandpit!' He began to work his way back up the tunnel. 'Come on! We can't stay here—if all that chanting starts again we might find ourselves feeding larvae for ever!'

'Well, just until the SWITCH spray wears off and we suddenly burst through the nest, back to our usual size!' said Danny.

'Danny, we're right down underneath the paving slabs! If we suddenly shoot up to full size we'll crack our heads open!' shuddered Josh. 'Come on—we can't stay here a minute longer!'

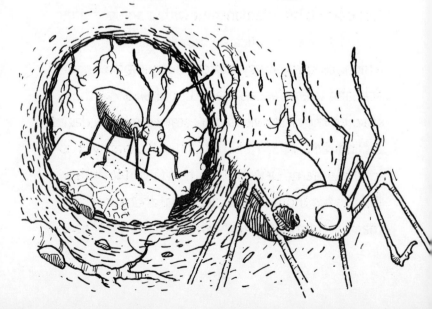

Danny hurried after his brother who was running over a shiny piece of glass, wrapped in winding grass roots. The glass sparkled in the narrow shaft of light that fed down from the nest entrance. Josh stopped.

Danny cannoned into him. 'COME ON, JOSH! YOU SAID WE'VE GOT TO GET OUT FAST!'

'Yes, but . . . ' Josh was peering down at the glass that glimmered up between the roots. 'This . . . this is . . . ' He thought he could make out a tiny turtle peering up at him. It was stirring up a memory. What about? He shook his head and scurried after Danny. Clearly all the ant chanting was driving him a bit mad. What would a tiny turtle be doing in an ants' nest?

They found their way out by following the scent of the air above them, but as soon as they reached the nest exit, Danny started to look dazed.

The 'ON. MUST FEED YOUNG,' chant was so loud out here. 'DANNY! DON'T LISTEN!' yelled Josh as his brother started to turn and rejoin the marching ants. 'DANNY! SING! SING WITH ME!'

Danny looked back at his brother and Josh started singing:

'Happy ant day to you!
Happy ant day to you!'

Danny joined in:

'Happy ant day, dear anty . . .
Have some more aphid poo!'

'YES—AGAIN!' shouted Josh and by the time they'd sung it through three times they were away from the long line of chanting ants, over a bridge of hairy green moss to the next slab and running towards the sandpit.

For a few seconds it seemed as if they were clear but then there was a thundering sensation and a stampede almost swept them off their feet. This ant queue was much less ordered and the chanting was wild and excited. 'Sweet! Sweet! Sweet! Sweet!' Danny and Josh found themselves carried along, towards something which filled the air with an even more sugary smell than the aphids.

'LOOK!' gasped Josh.

A wide lake lay before them, gleaming red in the sun and sending out the tantalizing smell. 'What is it?' murmured Danny.

'Whatever it is, it's sweet!' said Josh. All around him the ants were saying the same, 'Sweet! Sweet! Sweet! Sweet!' And they were all clustering around the edges and gleefully drinking from it. Across the middle of the lake, Josh could make out a very long wooden walkway, which some of the ants were scurrying along to get to the rosy syrup beneath it. It was tipping sideways rather dangerously. Josh suddenly declared, 'I know what it is! I know!'

'What?' said Danny. 'It smells amazing. Shall we have some?'

'No, it's too dangerous,' said Josh. 'Look!' And he waved his feelers towards two or three ants who had become trapped in the gloopy red liquid and were struggling hopelessly. 'They're never getting out of it. You've killed them.'

'Me? What are you on about?'

'It's your fault. You left half of your ice lolly there on the slab this morning. You ate the top bit and then left the strawberry bit still on the stick. So it's melted and now it's a sugar lake feeding frenzy. Ants will drown in it! They always do . . . '

Danny gulped. 'But they seemed so sensible before—so organized. Now they're going bonkers!'

He was right. Hundreds of ants were now charging to the lake. It looked like some kind of wild pop festival going on as they clambered over each other and shoved one another aside to get to the front.

'Sugar. Drives them nuts,' sighed Josh. 'Especially in the summer. You want to meet a few thousand ants? Just drop an ice lolly on the ground and wait. Crowds of spaced out sugar zombies who can't think straight. It's nearly as bad as our last birthday party.'

Danny felt bad. 'Come on,' he said, fighting his way back through the crowds of sugar crazed ants. 'We've got to get to the sandpit.'

'We're nearly at the edge of the slab,' yelled Josh. 'We just have to go past those old bricks that Dad put there.' The angle of red bricks had been cemented to the corner of the slab when Dad decided to make a barbecue. He hadn't done any more yet, so the bricks weren't very high. Unless you happened to be an ant. Now they loomed up like great tower blocks.

'Could go over them,' said Danny, as they drew closer. 'We can run up walls, no problem.'

'No, might get seen by a bird,' warned Josh. At least against the speckled grey of the paving slab they didn't stand out that much—but they would on red brick. 'Better go round.'

'OK, but we—' Danny stopped, because Josh had stopped. Josh was standing still and waving his feelers in the air. There was a big, rumbly, crackly feeling coming in through his antennae. Something big, rumbly, crackly . . . and hot. Very hot. An incredibly bright light flashed in their eyes.

'WHAT'S THAT?' shouted Danny. 'Josh—what is it?'

Josh stared back at Danny and his feelers quivered. 'I don't like this. I don't like this at all . . .'

Fry Up, Anyone?

'Smell it!' whispered Josh, sending great big waves of fear out through his scent squirting gear. 'It smells . . . like . . . burning.'

There was another bright flash and then they saw it. Something truly terrifying. A huge, brilliant, blindingly white pillar of fire. It was hitting the edge of the paving stone on the far side and they could sense panic among the ant colony they had just run away from. The terrible rumbling and burning was getting louder and stronger and Josh and Danny could see the pillar of fire moving from left to right, tilting at an angle, like a tornado, but not so shaky. Little pops and bursts of flame kept going off under it. Danny didn't want to think about what they were.

'What is it?' gasped Josh. 'What could be

making that happen? It's vaporizing everything in its path!'

Danny gulped and squinted up. Above them— high, high up in the sky, was a round glow, like the sun. Shooting out from the round glow was the pillar of fire. A dim shape loomed up somewhere beyond it. 'OH NO!' shrieked Danny. 'I know what it is! I know what it is! Josh! Don't stand there looking! RUN! WE'VE GOT TO RUN BEFORE HE SEES US!'

'He?' spluttered Josh as he legged it along behind Danny as fast as he could. 'Who's he?'

'It's Tarquin!' shouted back Danny.

'Tarquin? With a death ray? Who made him a god?'

'YOU did!' Danny reached the bottom of the red brick tower. 'When you let him pick up your magnifying glass! If he likes picking legs off things, I bet he's into frying things too. He's making the sun shine through the glass like a laser and frying everything that moves!'

'Oh no!' wailed Josh, spinning round as he reached his brother and taking in the terrible sight behind them. 'It's coming this way! He must have seen us!'

The crackling, smoking, white-hot beam wandered off to the left for a second, exploding something which looked like a poor little beetle, and then it moved relentlessly towards the brick wall corner that Josh and Danny were now backed into.

'Quick—we've got to run around the bricks and hide!' squeaked Josh.

'No—up and over! It's quicker!' yelled Danny. 'I don't care about the birds! We've got a death ray to worry about.'

He scrambled up the wall as fast as his three pairs of legs could carry him. Josh hurried up alongside him, but, glancing backwards, he could see it was hopeless. The death ray was speeding across the slab, heading straight for them. Any second now, one of them would be toast. And then the other.

'If he gets me first just keep running!' gasped Danny, also looking back over his shoulder. But the beam, as it got closer, was big enough to get them both. It swept up the wall, sending up a plume of hot, fine, red-brick dust. 'Oh no—we're done for,' wailed Danny and scrunched up into a ball on the edge of the brick. 'Bye bye, Josh—you've been a great brother . . . for a freaky little bug boffin.'

Josh scrunched up into a ball as well. 'Bye, Danny,' he gulped, sadly. 'You too . . . for a skateboard nut.'

The Heat is On/Off/On

THWACK!

'You nasty little tick!' Petty Potts slammed her net down over Tarquin's head. 'Are you really setting fire to innocent insects?'

Tarquin squawked with rage, dropped the magnifying glass onto the slabs, and struggled to get the net off his head. 'Get off! Get it off me, you horrid old woman! My mother will have the police on to you, I tell you.'

'Murderer,' muttered Petty, keeping the net firmly in place and waving a small torch-like device at the paving slab.

'They're only ants!'

Petty gulped. It was ants she was looking for. Her SWITCHee detector was bleeping off the scale. Now she was certain that Josh and Danny had been SWITCHed—and very likely barbecued. Which would be a little awkward. Shoving Tarquin out of the way, she knelt to peer at the bricks where the loathsome child had been directing the magnifying glass. She could just about make out two of the little creatures, cowering close together on the top edge. Could that be Josh and Danny? Could it? If so, they should be about to return to their proper shape any moment now, judging by her calculations. She turned off the SWITCHee detector and checked her watch.

'GET THIS OFF ME!' shouted Tarquin, again, still struggling pathetically with the net.

Petty flicked it off the boy. 'Go—shoo, you repulsive little gargoyle!' she told him, and Tarquin ran away, much to her relief. Now, were those two really Josh and Danny? Or was that just wishful thinking?

'Danny!' whispered Josh, unscrunching a little.

A cloud of hot brick dust swirled around him, stinging his eyes. 'Danny? Are you there?'

Danny looked out from his own scrunch and waggled his feelers shakily. 'Yes. I'm here. What happened?'

'It's gone! The death ray—it's gone!'

They stared all around them. There was no sign of the death ray.

'Phew-hoo!' hooted Danny, running over to Josh and doing a high five with him, with one feeler. 'We're not little piles of anty ash!'

'It's gone,' sighed Josh. 'We're safe.'

'Josh—Danny—is that you?' whispered Petty, screwing up her eyes and trying to see. Oh, here was the magnifying glass. That would help.

Considering she was a genius, Petty had occasional moments of being very, very, stupid. This was one now. She picked up the glass and held it over the two ants.

'AAAAAAAAAAAAAAAAAAAHHHHH!' screamed Josh and Danny as a blast of white heat suddenly hit them.

Oops

Petty was just beginning to realize that she was in fact killing the little ants she was hoping to help, when she was walloped in the face.

It was Danny who bashed her spectacles sideways and nearly flattened her nose. To be fair, he was just about to perish in a sea of flame when he abruptly returned to human form, so you couldn't blame him for lashing out a bit. The sea of flame did cause a slight mark on his knee, he later discovered.

Josh didn't smack anyone in the face. He just sprawled into the sandpit, where the blaze which had started on his right eyebrow was instantly put out.

'Oh! Oh! Oh! What a relief!' gasped Petty, fanning her face and swaying on her knees.

'Give me that!' Danny grabbed the magnifying glass and shoved it safely into his trouser pocket.

'It wasn't me trying to incinerate you!' protested Petty. 'I was just trying to find you and save you. Sorry it got a bit hot, though. I forgot about that magnified sunlight business for a few seconds there. No—the one who was trying to kill you was that ghastly child from round the corner.'

'What—*that* ghastly child?' said Josh standing up as Tarquin came back into the garden holding on to their mum's hand. He was looking wounded and sulky.

'Now, now, boys—Tarquin says you won't play with him,' said their mum. 'Oh, hello, Miss Potts.'

'Hello, dear,' said Petty standing up. 'Just looking at insects with your sons. I'm sure Tarquin is very welcome to join in. I'm off now—see you all later.'

And she hurried out of the garden with her SWITCHee detector, whistling with relief.

'No, he's not welcome,' said Josh. 'He just tried to kill us.'

Mum looked astonished. 'Really, boys, don't be so silly! What possible harm could little Tarquin do?' Little Tarquin smirked at them from under her arm.

'Well, if he'd got the chance he'd have pulled our legs off,' said Danny.

Mum laughed. 'You boys! Really! Here—I've brought some ice lollies for you all.' She gave them to Danny to hand out and went back into the house.

Danny grinned. He'd had an idea. He whispered to Josh as Tarquin ripped off his ice lolly wrapper and began slurping noisily. 'Shall we?' said Danny and Josh grinned back and nodded.

'Come on then,' said Danny. 'Let's sit here.' He led Tarquin over to sit on the paving slabs. As they walked Danny mashed his own ice lolly in one hand and let it drip onto the ground.

They all sat down. Danny melted more ice lolly while Josh kept Tarquin talking. Soon the sweet little yellow blobs made a pathway from a crumbly bit of soil at the edge of the slab—right up to their visitor's trouser legs and a little way inside. Then Danny shuffled closer to Tarquin and patted him on the back a few times, in a friendly, sticky way.

Tarquin didn't notice the mad sugar pop festival for quite a while. Not until it had got up across his jacket, scurried down inside his collar, and marched some way up his trouser leg.

'Who was screeching?' asked Mum a few minutes later, as she emerged from the house with Tarquin's mum.

'Is that my Tarquin, doing a little dance down the garden?' said Tarquin's mum.

'Nothing to worry about,' said Josh, with a happy smile.

'He's just got ants in his pants,' said Danny.

Nest Quest

When Tarquin had at last gone home with his mother, wearing a spare pair of Danny's shorts and crying loudly, Mum brought a cup of tea and some little fondant cakes out to them in the garden.

'Just to say thanks,' she said, handing them the tray as they sat on the garden bench. 'For trying. He's an annoying boy. Gives you heartburn.'

'You'll never know,' mumbled Danny, through a mouthful of cake.

Josh picked up the pink-iced sponge cube and stared at it as Mum went back indoors.

'Well go on, then,' said Danny. 'You love French Fancies.'

Josh raised his eyes up above the cake and stared at Danny, a slow smile spreading over his face.

'Now I know what I saw in the ants' nest!' he breathed.

'Yes,' said Danny. 'Ants. A lot of them.'

'Not just ants! I saw a tiny turtle too!'

'A tiny turtle too?' echoed Danny, wondering if Josh had decided to start making up funny songs. 'A tiddly turtle too . . . having a piddly poo?' he ventured.

Josh sprang to his feet and slammed the cake down on the plate. 'DANNY! I KNOW WHERE ANOTHER REPTOSWITCH CUBE IS!' And he began to run towards the paving slabs.

'COME ON! Petty's going to get another of her missing cubes back today! That'll be four out of six. Maybe that will be enough to crack the reptile SWITCH code. You never know!'

At the slabs they peered down into the crumbly brown nests in the cracks. 'I saw sparkly glass in the ants' nest tunnel, just before we ran back out,' explained Josh. 'And while I was looking into it I saw a turtle looking back up at me! It couldn't have been a real turtle—not in an ants' nest. It must be a hologram! A hologram in another one of Petty's missing cubes!'

He poked his fingers down into the nest, scattering dozens of panicked ants. 'Here! This is where we came out, I'm sure. Danny, help me get the slab up!'

'What are you two doing?' called Mum, looking out of the kitchen window.

'Just looking at an ants' nest,' called back Danny.

'Oh, that reminds me,' said Mum, and disappeared back through the window.

The slab was heavy but between them Josh and Danny managed to prise the edge up and lift it away. Underneath, a secret world was revealed—a flat grey plain of soil and grit and roots, with centipedes and woodlice fleeing across it as the daylight struck them. A complicated network of passages wriggled across the surface and scores of ants were running along them in a frenzy.

Josh and Danny knew that the tunnels went much deeper than this. 'How far down was the cube, then?' asked Danny.

'Can't be that deep—maybe ten centimetres . . . ?' guessed Josh. 'Look—there's the main entrance.'

He pointed to a larger hole, through which a long chain of ants was hurrying.

A shadow fell across them. Josh and Danny glanced up and there stood Mum. She was holding a glinting deadly weapon in her hand. A kettle.

Steam rose from its spout in menacing curls.

'Mind out,' said Mum. 'I've been meaning to do this all week. We've got far too many ants.'

'NOOOOOOO!!' screamed Josh and Danny, both together.

Mum blinked. She had expected Josh to protest a bit—but Danny? He didn't even like creepy-crawlies! She'd poured boiling water on nests before and he'd never batted an eyelid!

'You can't!' cried Josh. 'It's cruel! You'll wipe out an entire family and all their babies.'

'DON'T DO IT, MUM!' begged Danny.

Mum stepped back, shrugging. One steaming splash of water hit the nest and left a crater of hot mud. 'All right! All right!' she said. 'But don't blame me if you get ants in your pants like Tarquin!'

'We won't mind!' said Danny.

At last Mum went away and they breathed a huge sigh of relief. It was one thing to wipe out a nest of ants when you'd only just noticed them by your toes—quite another thing when you'd met them all and been round their house.

'OK, I'll be careful,' said Josh, prodding his fingers gently and slowly down through the main entrance. After only a few seconds, as the crumbly earth gave way, he felt a cold, hard angle of glass. In a moment he had seized it and wiggled it out of the embrace of the grass roots.

He knelt back and held it up to the light. One perfect glass cube, with a tiny, delicate hologram of a turtle inside it. He and Danny stared at each other, grinning excitedly. Then they leapt to their feet and tore down the side passage. Seconds later they were hammering on Petty's front door.

Petty Potts pulled them into her hallway and slammed the door, and then she took the cube from Josh's hand and stared at it, thrilled.

'Where was it?' she whispered.

'In an ants' nest in our garden,' said Josh. 'We would never have found it if we hadn't been turned into ants ourselves.'

'Oh yes,' said Danny, suddenly remembering. 'What were you thinking of, giving SWITCH spray to Tarquin?'

'I didn't give it to him, you donkey!' said Petty, but she was still smiling mistily into the cube. 'He just grabbed it when I left it on the wall for ten seconds.'

'You've got to be more careful,' said Josh.

'I am careful,' insisted Petty. 'And anyway, if you hadn't been turned into ants, we would never have got this back!'

They didn't bother to go on arguing because she was too entranced by the cube to pay any attention. She walked into the kitchen and got two boxes down from a high shelf. One was red velvet and one was green velvet. The red one, as she opened it, revealed a set of six perfect glass cubes. The BUGSWITCH cubes. Their six holograms contained the six parts of the code for making BUGSWITCH spray.

Now Petty opened the green box. In this lay three cubes and three empty dents. Petty pressed the fourth cube into its dent and sighed happily.

'Just two more to find!' she murmured. 'Two more and the REPTOSWITCH code will be mine again! Mine! MINE!'

She glanced at Josh and Danny and coughed. 'I mean . . . ours.' She smiled at them. 'And when it's complete, you two will be the first humans on earth to know how it feels to be a reptile! An alligator! A giant lizard! A python! Whatever you want! I will be able to make the spray . . .'

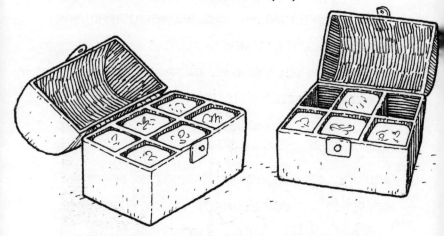

'Will it make us rich?' wondered Danny. Danny liked money.

'Of course,' said Petty. 'But more importantly, it will make us the most famous scientists in the world!'

A shadow moved in the passage which ran past Petty's kitchen window. She flinched and went to stare outside. 'Did you see that?' she whispered.

'What? It was probably just a cat,' said Josh.

Petty turned away from the window and stared at them both. 'You ought to know . . . ' she said, her eyes glittering, ' . . . that the closer we get to finding the REPTOSWITCH code, the more dangerous it could get.'

Danny blinked. 'Look, we've been nearly eaten by a centipede and then burnt alive by a magnifying glass today. I think we know how dangerous it gets.'

'No, I mean . . . we're probably being watched.' Petty flicked a glance back over her shoulder. 'By them . . .'

'Them?' said Josh.

'They have a file on me,' said Petty. 'I might have been expelled from the government's secret laboratories, but they've always been watching me. The postman, the milkman, the lady who delivers fish . . . any one of them could be a government spy working for Victor Crouch. He might have burnt my memory out, but he'll always have someone on the look out, just in case. Watching and waiting. Waiting for a sign that my work goes on! He failed to steal it properly before, then burnt out my memory before he realized his stupid mistake—that the notes he stole from me were all faked. He will always wonder if it's possible for me to start again. And, just in case, he will always have someone watching . . .'

'O . . . K,' said Josh. 'Time for us to go home now. Byeeeee.'

'I tell you! They're like ants! They're everywhere!' insisted Petty, snapping the velvet boxes shut. 'Be on your guard! Tell me if you see anything suspicious! Anything at all . . .'

'She's bonkers,' said Danny, as Petty closed her front door and they walked down the front garden path. 'Every bonkers person thinks the government is spying on them.'

'Yep,' said Josh.

Across the road, the man emptying the postbox finished filling up his sack. Then, when nobody seemed to be looking, he took out a pair of binoculars and trained them on Petty Potts's house . . .

DIARY ENTRY *605.8
SUBJECT: FOUR PARTS OF THE CODE NOW FOUND!

Whoever would have thought it? Danny and Josh got turned into ants today, quite by mistake. Of course, it was useful for my research and I will get them to tell me the details tomorrow.

But MUCH more importantly, while they were ants, they went into a nest in their garden and found the fourth REPTOSWITCH cube!!! I am now two-thirds of the way back to getting the reptile morphing code!!!

I always knew that I would have hidden the cubes close to home, but I may never remember exactly where. I just hope that the final two are discovered soon, before one of Victor Crouch's spies gets wind of how Josh and Danny are helping.

$$\frac{4 \times \pi^2}{OS - 7^*} \searrow \frac{\boxed{P_2}}{0.8} \times \frac{\sqrt{6}^2 \, 0/9}{9 \cdot \sqrt{5}^+} = \frac{4 \cdot 198}{4 \cdot 197}{(548)} \rightarrow$$

$$\searrow \qquad \rightarrow$$

I dreamed of Crouch last night. He was staring at me and waving his spiky black little finger and I was throwing lizards at him, but he didn't look shocked. Well, a man with no eyebrows can't really look shocked.

But that's not important. The important thing is my genius move to get Josh and Danny on board is still working out well. After all, who is ever going to believe that two eight year olds are helping me on the project?

But I have had to warn them about the spies. I don't think they believed me. I might have to show them some evidence of my life before, when I worked with Victor in the government's secret underground labs. And I should probably show them his photograph. They need to be on their guard now.

They may only be children, but that wouldn't stop Victor if he ever found out what they knew. That wouldn't stop him at all . . . ?

REMEMBER →

$$\frac{60}{OUP \cdot \pi} \rightarrow \cancel{\phi} \rightarrow \frac{1}{2}St^2$$

S.W.I.T.C.H

→

PLACES TO VISIT

Want to brush up on your bug knowledge?
Here's a list of places with special areas dedicated
to creepy-crawlies.

Liverpool Museum
http://www.liverpoolmuseums.org.uk/wml/
naturalworld/bughouse/

Marwell Wildlife Park
http://www.marwell.org.uk/

Natural History Museum
http://www.nhm.ac.uk/

Remember, you don't need
to go far to find your favourite
bugs. Why not venture out
into your garden or the
park and see how many
different creatures
you can spot.

WEBSITES

Find out more about nature and wildlife
using the websites below.

http://www.bbc.co.uk/cbbc/wild/

http://www.nhm.ac.uk/kids-only/

http://kids.nationalgeographic.com/

http://www.switch-books.co.uk/

Another exciting adventure awaits . . .

Ali Sparkes
Winner of the Blue Peter
Book of the Year

Illustrated by
Ross Collins

S.W.I.T.C.H.

SERUM WHICH INSTIGATES TOTAL CELLULAR HIJACK

Crane Fly Crash

Something In the
Hair Tonight

A horrific murder was about to take place in a dark alley. The victim fluttered helplessly in the shadow of a terrifying spiked weapon which pounded against the wall, missing only by inches.

The murderer was cold. Unfeeling. Able to kill with a single blow and then turn away without a moment's remorse. The victim knew time was nearly up. One more attack and there would be nothing left but a mashed corpse.

The spiked weapon swung forward.

'Jenny! Stop it!' Josh leaped across his big sister's bedroom floor and grabbed her arm just before it swung the hairbrush down again.

'Hey! Get off!' yelled Jenny, trying to shake her little brother off her arm. But now his twin,

101

Danny, came running in too, with an excited whoop, and threw himself at her other arm.

'You're a murderer!' shrieked Josh. 'Killing innocent moths! How could you?'

The poor moth in question flapped limply up the wall from behind Jenny's bed and bumbled against the windowpane, trying to get away.

'It's just a *moth*, Josh! Not a cat or a dog or a person!' snapped Jenny, her long blonde hair whipping about as she wrestled with her brothers.

'Just because it's small, doesn't mean it doesn't have feelings,' said Danny, now climbing onto his sister's back and making her spin round furiously.

'Danny! *Get off!*' Jenny whacked her elbows back, and Danny fell onto her bed. Josh had let his sister go and was now peering closely at the brown moth. Jenny shook her head at Danny. 'You don't even *like* creepy-crawlies. You go nuts if one lands on *you*!'

'True,' shrugged Danny. 'They can be creepy— but they are quite amazing too. I should know. I've been a spider, you know. And a bluebottle. And a grasshopper. Oh—and an ant. That was amazing!'

'Yeah, right,' snorted Jenny. 'Well, you always creep *me* out, anyway!'

Danny laughed. He knew Jenny couldn't possibly believe what he'd just said. Even though it was true. He and Josh *had* been all those creatures over the summer, ever since they stumbled into the secret laboratory in next door's garden and discovered something incredible.

Their neighbour, Petty Potts, might seem like a batty old lady, but it turned out she was a genius scientist who had invented SWITCH—a spray which could turn you into a creepy-crawly. Only Danny and Josh knew her secret since the day when they had accidentally got sprayed and turned into spiders. They'd been afraid of her at first but now they were helping her by searching for some special missing cubes. They'd got four already, but if they found just two more, Petty would have the code to make a new SWITCH spray—which could change you into a reptile. They could find out how it felt to be snake, or a lizard, or even an alligator!

'You don't *have* to kill him, you know,' Josh told Jenny, still examining the moth. 'All you have to do is open the window.'

'I've tried *that*,' huffed Jenny. 'But it just keeps flying back in!'

'You need to turn your light off,' explained Josh, reaching over and switching off Jenny's bedside lamp. 'Moths get confused and think it's the moon and keep flying towards it.' He eased open the window, blew gently on the moth, and smiled as it flew away into the night. 'Off you go, hawky!' he called after it. 'Go get your tea!' He closed the

104

window and glanced back into the room where
Danny was squirming on the bed with Jenny's foot
on his head. 'It's a hawk moth. They feed on nectar
by moonlight. Isn't that sweet? And they can smell
their girlfriends from miles and miles away.'

'Eeeuurgh,' commented Danny.

'Yeah, thanks for the biology lesson, you freaky
little bug boffin,' said Jenny, finally releasing Danny
and switching her lamp back on. 'Now get out of
my room, both of you. I've got to get ready to go
out.' And she flounced to her mirror and started
to brush her hair with the deadly weapon, while
rummaging through all the bottles and pots of hair
and make-up stuff. 'MUM!' she bellowed, ignoring
them. 'Where's my hair spray?'

Mum didn't answer—she was singing along to the radio in the kitchen—but the doorbell rang as Josh and Danny mooched out of Jenny's room, and shrugged at each other . . . Jenny was *such* a teenager.

Danny slid down the banister and leaped off at the bottom step, landing with a thud by the front door and opening it a second later.

Standing on the doorstep was Petty Potts. As soon as she saw Danny, and Josh stepping up behind him, she darted her eyes left and right behind her thick spectacles and hissed, 'Excellent! The very people I  was hoping for!' Her tweedy old hat was pulled down low over her face and the collar of her old trench coat was turned up. She looked as if she was pretending to be a spy.

'Shhhhhh!' said Petty, not coming into the house but leaning closer to them. 'Now listen— this is very important. Very important.'

'What is?' said Danny.

'Hush! Shhhh!' Petty pulled her coat tight across her chest and frowned at Danny. 'I need your help—but only you two must know!'

Josh sighed. Sometimes he thought Petty didn't even realize that she was an old age pensioner and he and Danny were still in junior school. She behaved as if they were all the same age. 'What is it, Petty?' he asked, warily. Whenever they got involved with Petty Potts they always seemed to end up uncomfortably close to being dead.

Petty glanced around again. 'I am going away to a conference in Berlin,' she said, in a low voice. 'A very important conference.'

'Are you going to show off your SWITCH spray?' asked Danny.

'No! No! Not yet.' Petty looked quite alarmed. 'The world of science is not ready. I can't reveal my secrets now! Not yet. But—if something were to happen to me . . . ' She peered at them, slowly nodding her head. 'Oh yes—something *could* happen to me, and then my work might never ever be known! And that—*that*—would be a tragedy!'

107

'Do you think someone's after you then?' whispered Josh.

Petty squinted at him. 'What?'

'You know,' said Josh. 'I mean—you've said before that you think people are spying on you, but do you think they're actually out to get you? Like in films?'

'Good grief, no,' said Petty, as if she thought Josh was simple-minded. 'I just mean that I might get run over by a bus or something. And of course, that could happen at any time! Anyway, just in case it does, while I am away, I want you to keep this!' And she pulled a plastic spray bottle out of her coat; the kind with a squirty button on the top and a little plastic cap over the button.

'We don't want that!' gasped Danny, backing away.

'Oh for heaven's sake! It's perfectly safe—all sealed tight,' said Petty. 'Just pop it under your bed or something and keep it until I get back. Then if I *don't* come back for any reason, you can take it to *New Scientist* magazine and reveal my genius to the world.'

'Petty,' said Josh, 'have you ever noticed that we're not grown-ups? I mean . . . you do realize that we're only eight, don't you?'

'What's that got to do with anything?' said Petty, thrusting the bottle into Josh's hands and then turning and running back down the path. 'See you next week, all being well! Take care, now. And keep searching for the cubes!'

Josh and Danny closed the door and stared at the bottle. 'Wonder which type of spray it is,' muttered Danny. 'Maybe . . . bee or wasp. Or centipede . . . '

'We are not going to find out,' said Josh. Danny nodded. As exciting as their creepy-crawly adventures had been, they had both been nearly eaten far too many times now to want to have a go with Petty's latest spray.

It was still hard to believe, but Petty Potts had created SWITCH spray in the underground lab in her garden, using a secret formula she had worked out during her years with the government in a top secret science department. She might be there still if her so-called friend, the eyebrow-less Victor

Crouch, had not tried to steal her work and then wipe out her memory.

His plan was foiled, though, because Petty had suspected foul play, put a fake formula in her work desk—and hidden the *real* secret SWITCH formula inside six little glass cubes. Then she had recreated it at home when bits of her memory began to come back. It really worked. Josh and Danny ought to know. They'd been SWITCHed four times now.

'Come on,' said Josh, heading up the stairs. 'Let's take this up to our room and find a place to hide it. She's better off not having it, probably. She sprays way too much of this stuff around.'

'We really should just try to stay away from her! Not answer the door next time,' said Danny.

'I know,' said Josh. 'But . . . if we ever *did* find all her other lost secret formula cubes . . . well . . . ' He bit his lip but his eyes shone. Petty had made a second secret formula—to create a spray which could switch them into reptiles—and put it into another six cubes. Only . . . she'd lost them. So far they'd only found four. Without the last two it could never work.

'Imagine,' continued Josh. 'I could be a snake!'

'I could be an alligator!' said Danny.

'*If* we ever find the last two REPTOSWITCH cubes . . . ' sighed Josh. Petty had begged them both to search for her, but who knew where the missing cubes could be? The first four they'd found around the gardens and houses in their neighbourhood, but they might never find the last two. Petty had hidden them too well and that bit of her memory—about where they were—had not come back.

'I could be a giant tree lizard . . . ' went on Danny.

Suddenly something swung down from the top of the banister. 'OI! You little monsters! I knew you'd been messing with my stuff! Gimme my hairspray now!' And Jenny swiped the bottle out of Josh's hands before he could even squeak.

'HEY NO! NO! JENNY, THAT'S NOT YOURS!' shouted Josh. In reply, Jenny just slammed her bedroom door. Josh and Danny stood on the stairs and stared at each other in horror. Then they hurtled up to the landing and across to Jenny's room.

'JENNY! DON'T USE THAT! DON'T SPRAY IT!' they shrieked, in utter panic, crashing her door wide open.

'OUT of my room!' shouted Jenny. She had taken the plastic cap off the spray bottle and was holding it up to her swept-back hair.

'Jenny! Please!' begged Josh, feeling his head reel with panic. 'DO NOT USE THAT SPRAY! It's not what you think it is!'

'Oh ha-ha!' said Jenny. 'Very funny.' And she sprayed a great cloud of SWITCH all over her head.

FUN AND GAMES

There are more games for you to play and
download free on the S.W.I.T.C.H. website.

www.switch-books.co.uk

Word search

Search for the hidden words listed below:

PIDDLE	JOSH
APHID	LASER
DANNY	LARVAE
ANT	TARQUIN
ICE LOLLY	CENTIPEDE

S	P	I	D	D	L	E	T	A	E
H	F	I	I	A	T	W	N	D	O
J	D	H	N	N	Q	H	E	R	D
X	P	R	F	N	A	P	I	T	N
A	B	F	A	Y	I	R	S	L	I
N	O	M	S	T	G	E	O	A	U
T	D	C	N	H	U	S	T	R	Q
M	J	E	I	S	Y	A	U	V	R
I	C	E	L	O	L	L	Y	A	A
Y	P	H	K	J	O	N	T	E	T

Spot the difference

These pictures *look* the same.
But can you spot
seven differences?

Answers on page 122

True or false?

1) Some ants can carry up to 50 times their own weight

2) Ants are solitary creatures who prefer to live alone

3) Ants only eat meat

4) Every ant colony has a king ant

5) The Australian Bulldog ant has very powerful jaws
to kill its prey

6) The Giant Tiger centipede has yellow and black stripes
and lives in the jungle

7) Centipedes are vegetarians

8) Ants protect aphids from predators

9) Ants have no sense of smell

10) Ants have two sets of eyes

Answers on page 122

Maze

Can you help Josh and Danny
escape to the garden?

Answer on page 123

Are you a bug boffin?

Question 1)
HOW OLD IS TARQUIN?
A) Eight
B) Seven and three quarters
C) Seven and a half

Question 2)
HOW DO ANTS COMMUNICATE WITH EACH OTHER?
A) By making clicking sounds
B) By releasing chemicals into the air and by using their feelers
C) A complicated form of sign language, using their antennae and front two legs

Question 3)
HOW DO JOSH AND DANNY GET AWAY FROM THE CENTIPEDE?
A) They squirt formic acid in his face
B) Tarquin treads on the centipede by mistake and Josh and Danny run away
C) They hide under a rock until the centipede loses interest

Question 4)
DANNY TRIES A NEW FOOD AFTER HE'S BEEN TURNED INTO AN ANT WHICH HE DESCRIBES AS TASTING LIKE GOLDEN SYRUP. WHAT IS IT?
A) A juicy aphid
B) A succulent leaf
C) Aphid poo

Question 5)
WHERE DO JOSH AND DANNY FIND THE REPTOSWITCH CUBE?
A) In an ants' nest in their back garden
B) In Tarquin's trouser pocket
C) On top of the garden wall

Question 6)
WHAT DOES TARQUIN USE TO TRY AND KILL THE ANTS IN THE BACK GARDEN?
A) A water pistol
B) His boot
C) A magnifying glass

Question 7)
WHAT SYMBOL IS THE HOLOGRAM INSIDE THE REPTOSWITCH CUBE JOSH AND DANNY FIND?
A) A lizard
B) A turtle
C) A snake

Question 8)
HOW DO JOSH AND DANNY END UP GETTING TURNED INTO ANTS?
A) Tarquin sprays them with SWITCH spray
B) They spray themselves with SWITCH spray
C) Petty Potts puts some SWITCH formula in their drink

Answers on page 123

Answers

Word search (page 116)

S	P	I	D	D	L	E	T	A	E
H	F	I	I	A	T	W	N	D	O
J	D	H	N	N	Q	H	E	R	D
X	P	R	F	N	A	P	I	T	N
A	B	F	A	Y	I	R	S	L	I
N	O	M	S	T	G	E	O	A	U
T	D	C	N	H	U	S	T	R	Q
M	J	E	I	S	Y	A	U	V	R
I	C	E	L	O	L	L	Y	A	A
Y	P	H	K	J	O	N	T	E	T

Spot the difference (page 117)

True or False (page 118)

1) True
2) False
3) False
4) False
5) True
6) True
7) False
8) True
9) False
10) False

122

Answers

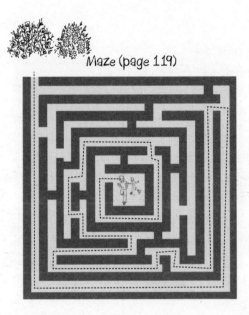

Maze (page 119)

Are you a bug boffin?
(page 121)
Answer 1) C
Answer 2) B
Answer 3) A
Answer 4) C
Answer 5) A
Answer 6) C
Answer 7) B
Answer 8) A

Give yourself a point for every question you got right.

6-8 POINTS — You are a real bug boffin! Nothing gets past you.

3-5 POINTS — You are SWITCHed on! You enjoy a good adventure.

0-2 POINTS — Oh dear, looks as if you need to brush up on your bug skills! Better luck next time!

About the author

Ali Sparkes grew up in the woods of Hampshire.
Actually, strictly speaking she grew up in a house
in Hampshire. The woods were great but lacked
basic facilities like sofas and a well stocked fridge.
Nevertheless, the woods were where she and
her friends spent much of their time and so Ali
grew up with a deep and abiding love of wildlife.
If you ever see Ali with a large garden spider on
her shoulder she will most likely be screeching
'AAAAAAAAAARRRRRGHGETITOFFME!'

Ali lives in Southampton with her husband and sons
and would never kill a creepy-crawly of any kind. They
are more scared of her than she is of them. (Creepy-
crawlies, not her husband and sons.)

Other books

in the  S.W.I.T.C.H. series

SERUM WHICH INSTIGATES TOTAL CELLULAR HIJACK

Ali Sparkes — Illustrated by Ross Collins

S.W.I.T.C.H.
SERUM WHICH INSTIGATES TOTAL CELLULAR HIJACK

Spider Stampede

Ali Sparkes — Illustrated by Ross Collins

S.W.I.T.C.H.
SERUM WHICH INSTIGATES TOTAL CELLULAR HIJACK

Fly Frenzy

Ali Sparkes — Illustrated by Ross Collins

S.W.I.T.C.H.
SERUM WHICH INSTIGATES TOTAL CELLULAR HIJACK

Grasshopper Glitch

Ali Sparkes — Illustrated by Ross Collins

S.W.I.T.C.H.
SERUM WHICH INSTIGATES TOTAL CELLULAR HIJACK

Crane Fly Crash

Ali Sparkes — Illustrated by Ross Collins

S.W.I.T.C.H.
SERUM WHICH INSTIGATES TOTAL CELLULAR HIJACK

Beetle Blast

Whether you're interested in insects
or terrified of tarantulas, you'll love the
S.W.I.T.C.H. website!

Find out more about the bugs in Josh
and Danny's adventures, enter fantastic
competitions, read the first chapters
of all of the S.W.I.T.C.H. books, and enjoy
creepy-crawly games and activities.

www.switch-books.co.uk